Rapunzel

First published in 2005 by
Franklin Watts
96 Leonard Street
London
EC2A 4XD

Franklin Watts Australia
45–51 Huntley Street
Alexandria
NSW 2015

A CIP catalogue record for this book is available
from the British Library.

ISBN 0 7496 6147 X (hbk)
ISBN 0 7496 6159 3 (pbk)

Series Editor: Jackie Hamley
Series Advisor: Dr Barrie Wade
Series Designer: Peter Scoulding

Printed in Hong Kong / China

For Andrew – H.R.

For Emilie – M.I.

Rapunzel

Retold by Hilary Robinson

Illustrated by Martin Impey

FRANKLIN WATTS
LONDON•SYDNEY

Once upon a time, there was a beautiful girl with long, golden hair.

Her name was Rapunzel.
A wicked witch hid her
in a tower with no door.

Rapunzel could not escape.
She was so bored that she
sang all day long.

To get into the tower the witch would cry:

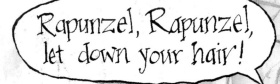

Rapunzel, Rapunzel, let down your hair!

Then she would climb up
Rapunzel's long hair.

One day a prince rode by.

He heard Rapunzel singing
and fell in love with her.

He watched how the witch
climbed into the tower.

Later, he called:

Rapunzel, Rapunzel, let down your hair!

The Prince climbed into the tower. Rapunzel soon fell in love with him. They planned her escape.

Rapunzel made a ladder
from some silk the Prince
had brought her.

Soon she would be able
to climb out of the tower.

But when the witch next
came to see her, Rapunzel
made a big mistake.

She cried: "Why are you
so much heavier than
the Prince?"

The witch was furious.

She cut off Rapunzel's hair.

Then she hid her in
the woods.

Later, the prince rode to
the tower. He called:

Rapunzel, Rapunzel,
let down your hair!

But when he climbed up
he saw ...

… the angry witch! "Away!" she cried and pushed him onto the thorns below.

The Prince's eyes were scratched by the thorns.
He couldn't see any more.

For two years he was lost
in the woods.

Then, one day, he heard
beautiful singing.
"Rapunzel!" he cried.

Rapunzel's tears of joy
helped the Prince to
see again.

The Prince led Rapunzel to his palace where they lived happily ever after.

Leapfrog has been specially designed to fit the requirements of the **National Literacy Strategy**. It offers real books for beginning readers by top authors and illustrators.

There are 31 Leapfrog stories to choose from: